# Lana's Day at Church

## by Linda Lockett

### Illustrations by Stephanie Anduro

LAL Innovations LLC

Copyright © 2023 by Linda Lockett
All rights reserved.
LCCN: 2023905764 (print)
ISBN: 979-8-9880681-0-5 (print)
ISBN: 979-8-9880681-1-2 (ebook)

Juvenile Fiction/People & Places/United States/African American & Black
Juvenile Fiction/Religious/Christian/Bedtime & Dreams
Juvenile Fiction/Girl/Women
Juvenile Fiction/Animals/General

Printed in the United States of America
www.lanasday.com

Book Illustrated by Stephanie Anduro

*Dedicated to and in Observance of*
*Prairie Chapel Missionary Baptist Church*
*248-Year Anniversary*
*and the Congregational Families:*
*Green, Harris, Jones, Brown, Ellis, Jennings and Tucker*

Grandma ties
with gentle care,
yellow satin ribbons
in Lana's hair.

Lana's on her way
to church today
to celebrate, worship,
sing and praise.

Now Lana is ready
to take a long ride
in the little red auto,
to the little wood church
in the countryside.

On down the road
little red auto passes by
little wood houses
with sittin' chairs and swings;

then up the hill
passing great big houses
with sweet smelling flowers
on tall Magnolia trees.

Little red auto
rides through Catfish Alley
where cafes are famous
for the most de-li-cious
fresh catfish, crispy and fried;

slow-cooked collard greens,
and sweet potato pies!

As the little red auto
cross the Tombigbee Bridge,
wheels are making, a very loud hum,
& under the bridge cafishes jump and grin.

In their watery voices to Lana they sing,
"Hello there Lana!
We are happy, to see you again.
Have a beautiful day,
at church my good friend!"

Little red auto on graveled road
kicking up pebbles and dust in breeze.
High on top of the Mississippi pine trees
cicadas make buzzing sounds,
so simple and so sweet,
in delightful harmony to Lana they sing,
"Hello there Lana!
We are happy, to see you again.
Have a beautiful day,
at church my good friend!"

Little red auto drives by cotton fields;
new rows of white cotton flowers
are swaying in the wind,
waiting to be plucked
when fully grown again.

Wheels are rolling up the muddy red road.
Cows are grazing on lush green sod.
They raise their heads, just to give a nod.

In their moo-ing voices, to Lana they sing,
"Hello there Lana!
We are happy, to see you again.
Have a beautiful day,
at church my good friend!"

Atop of the hill Lana arrives,
to the little wood church in the countryside.
Happy voices are gathered inside.

All eyes are on Sister Sallie
singing Mahalia's song,
'Move On Up a Little Higher,'
and the church folks join in;
they clap their hands to the music, and sing.

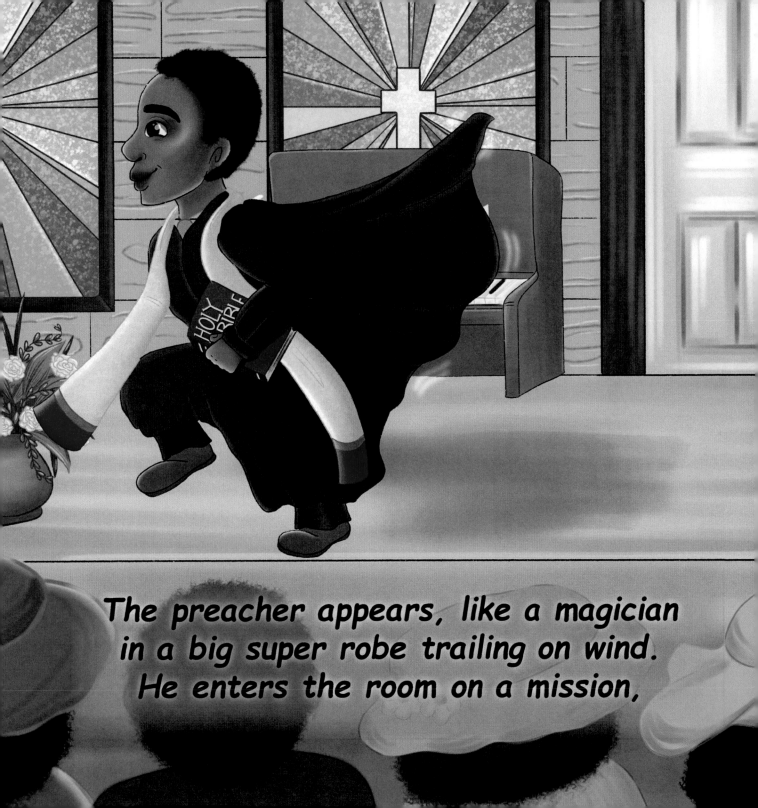

The preacher appears, like a magician
in a big super robe trailing on wind.
He enters the room on a mission,

preaching to all in-spi-ration
that "God is Love!"
The church rejoices, "Hal-le-lu-jah!"
"thank ye lawdy! A-A- Amen!"

The church sing songs, shout and praise,
circle walk, dance, and 'get happy,'
a time to gather, a time to celebrate,

on this beautiful, wonderful
Holy day inside,
the little wood church
in the countryside.

Now church has ended
with closing prayer A-A-Amen!
We all say our goodbyes,
give each other great big hugs,

until we meet here again
on another day inside
the little wood church,
in the countryside.

The little red auto is ready to go back down the path of the muddy red road. Lana waves goodbye to the cows on the hill, and to new cotton flowers standing in the fields.

She waves goodbye to the cicadas in the
trees, and to catfishes under the
Tombigbee Bridge.

Little red auto rolls down Catfish Alley,
by great big houses with tall Magnolia trees,
and pass little wood houses with sittin'
chairs and swings.

Now little red auto has arrived,
back to Lana's
little wood house again.

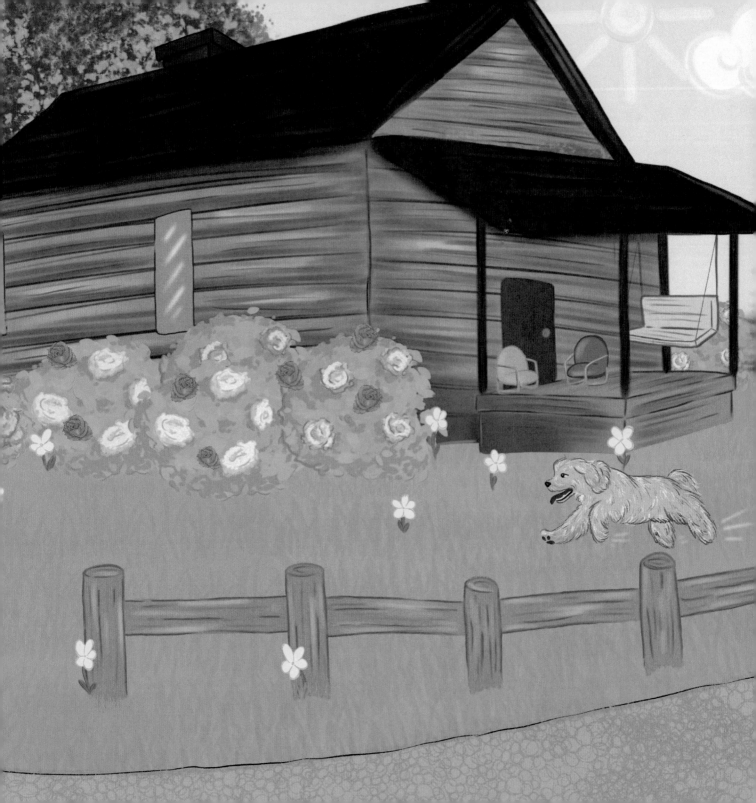

There from the middle of grandma's garden
a butterfly rests in Lana's hand.
As it shows off its colors
and spreads its shiny wings,
makes Lana smile and she begins to sing,
"Hello there, my little friend!
I am so happy to see you
fluttering in the wind,
on this beautiful, blessed day
when we celebrate inside,
at the little wood church
in the countryside."

## ABOUT THE AUTHOR

Linda Lockett is author of Lana's Day at Church which reflects her early childhood's rural Southern African American church experience. She is a higher education professor with an interest in politics and religion, and climate change. As a former pre-school teacher, she enjoys writing about happy events of childhood for young readers. Linda also writes non-fiction, science fiction, lyrics, and poetry.

Linda cares about the survival of plant and animal life as they are important for sustaining the environment. Lana's Day at Church highlights a few of the beautiful fauna and flora present in the North Mississippi region.

The state of Mississippi has annual and periodical cicadas. The periodical cicadas visit every 13 years. Cicadas are a food source for wasps.

The catfish is king in the state of Mississippi which produces the largest production of catfish in the United States.

Mississippi is one of the leading states with cotton fiber growth and production along with five other states.

The Mississippi state tree is the Southern magnolia. The state flower is the Magnolia. Before bees evolved the Magnolia flower encouraged pollination by beetles.

Look for more Lana's Day at Church book series at
Lanasday.com